MALCOLM WEBSTER, (ASPIRING) 5TH-GRADE WHIZ KID

DAKOTA B. KLAES

CHAPTER 1

"**M**alcolm!" my mom shrieked as she thrust her bony shoulder into my bedroom door, busting it open. "Dinner time, now!" The swinging wood pounded against my desk chair, causing my masterpiece to wobble.

"Mom!" I called back, desperate. "You're going to knock over the Mega Volcano!" I steadied the bottle of vinegar in my left hand and the box of baking soda in my right. Dazzling foam began to rise from within my homemade lava-lair. Frothy liquid, the color of all the best Starburst flavors mixed together, surged from the depths of my creation, ready to gurgle up, out, and everywhere.

"Science will have to wait," Mom told me. "I'm making salmon."

Seeming not to notice the imminent molten meltdown, she snatched the vinegar from my hand. "That's where this has been! You know my recipe needs vinegar," she lectured me. I turned to face her, forcing an apologetic smile, though I was still mostly paying attention to the impending eruption I had engineered.

"I'm not hungry," I lied. I'm always hungry. "Can't I just eat after my experiment?" I begged.

She stepped toward my desk. "You have to eat, Malcolm. Even a self-described boy genius like yourself needs nutrients to grow up strong. Salmon's loaded with the good fats."

Let me tell you something about the good fats. They aren't nearly as delicious as the bad fats. I can't even believe they have the same name. Totally misleading.

With a glimpse past her approaching shoulder, I saw that bubbles were rising from the pointy peak as fast as I could think. We were seconds from liftoff.

Unfortunately, Mom had not seemed to notice. She was standing right in the blast radius! "Can I come right back to this after I eat?" I asked, hoping to usher her toward safety.

She pondered my question, staring deep into my eyes. "Have you finished your homework yet?"

Homework. What a silly invention—mere busy-work designed to occupy the time of real intellectuals like yours truly. I prefer to focus my time on actual science, like when I built a solar oven using aluminum foil so that I could (a) try to win the Seventh-Grade Science Fair (as a fourth-grader, no biggie) and (b) cook late-night pizza rolls in my bedroom without waking anyone up via smoke detector.

"Homework? Eh," I paused to bide my time. I made a face like I'd never heard such a word, though this is a near-weekly discussion.

Just then, my salty suds tidal-waved out of the volcano!

Blowing upward with power and grace, like a beluga whale belly-flop, the splash was at least three times larger than any I'd ever pulled off before. A true miracle of modern science. I stood in awe.

However, it immediately became clear that I had not fully calibrated my calculations to include one potential outside factor: a mother, especially my own, standing directly inside the liquid's landing zone.

Whether it was too much baking soda or not the right type of vinegar, within an instant Mom's glasses, curly brown hair, and white dress-shirt were soaked in my homemade magma. She puffed orange and red bubbles from her lip. "Downstairs, now!"

Keys to losing an argument: having your latest science experiment blow up all over your opponent. Mom was not happy. I had to admit defeat.

Mega Volcano = Mega Fail. If we had one of those Days Since Last Accident signs, we'd have to reset it to 0 (from 1).

"And, no more experiments tonight! It's all home-work, Mister," she said.

"No experiments tonight?" I cried. "All of science will suffer!"

"You have a C+ in science class, honey," she said.

"Yeah, but I've got enthusiasm," I snapped back, looking down at the freshly stained carpet.

"I know you do, but, still, it's all books tonight. I know that final paper is coming up, and these exper-iments keep you from your actual schoolwork. And making friends. And ..." She'd lost me with mention of the final paper.

Ugh.

This was not just any paper. This was a mutant-sized, 10-page, single-spaced end-of-the-schoolyear paper that was dead-set on ruining my life. Why on Earth should I be subjected to this cruel and unusual punishment?

I'd do anything to get out of that beast. It was going to take up all my experiment time!

I snapped back into reality, knowing that I had to think quickly if I was going to get out of starting that paper tonight.

Mom stormed through my tiny bedroom, collecting anything that might be a potential "distraction" for the night's homework. I followed closely behind, apologizing rapid-fire and doing my best to clean up the mess with crinkled Taco King napkins.

As Mom disappeared down the hall, I stopped for a second to jot down some notes on today's findings. The scientific method does, of course, require extensive documentation of data. Sitting on the bed I'd already outgrown last year, I scribbled across the top of the page: Mega Volcano Experiment - next time maybe less baking soda and definitely less lava on mom. I plunked my notebook down on my now empty desk. Mom had cleared the area of all my precious science equipment: graduated cylinders, microscopes, and double chocolate chip brownie bites to fuel late-night hypothesizing. It was a sad sight. Everything was gone except my telescope, which must have been too bulky for even a grownup to move.

Before heading downstairs, I gazed through it one last time, knowing my days of scientific exploration might be numbered.

Before bed, I always like to stare up at the stars, and envision a world up there. Planets, black holes, starships, other intergalactic stuff I've studied but can't remember right now. Jedis. And, of course, aliens.

Sometimes, though, as I look out on the horizon, I can't help but catch a glimpse of my neighbor's house. The only problem is, my neighbor is my homeroom teacher, Mrs. Dawkins.

I mean right next door?! Come on, a kid needs a buffer zone!

She's a nice lady, as far as homeroom teachers go. But she was also the one who assigned that final paper, the fun-sucking, life-ruining one that Mom had been carrying on about. She couldn't be trusted.

I looked out, and saw Mrs. Dawkins alone at her kitchen counter. She was almost always by herself—grading homework, designing lesson plans, plotting new ways to destroy all that is fun and good in life, etc.

"What does a teacher even eat for dinner?" I wondered.

She reached up, and was barely able to reach the microwave. I'm already taller than Mrs. Dawkins, and I'm young for a fifth-grader (though, obviously, of above average intelligence). With a dainty gloved hand, always with those fancy things, she popped open the micro-wave door and removed what looked almost like a stack of soggy papers. She went in for her first bite of the mashed potatoey mush that had little black splotches on it like a newspaper that'd been left in the rain.

What the—? Gross. I felt like I was hallucinating. Not enough of the bad fats today. I gotta eat something.

I hustled downstairs to the dinner table.

We sat down for what Mom called a wholesome family dinner, which in my opinion was missing several key food groups: BBQ sauce, baby back ribs, regular cheese, nacho cheese …. Mom sat at the head of the table, where Dad would have sat, if he hadn't been in the accident last year. It still makes me sad to talk about it, so I just won't. That's called maturity. And, let's face it, I'm just not that brave.

Mom was still a little annoyed with me, but I thought the tie-dye hints on her dress shirt made it look a lot less boring. I even complimented her.

She smiled and passed me the salmon, which, though it definitely fell within the dreaded good fat category of foods, still looked better than what Mrs. D'd been eating next door. I ate what I could (two bites dipped in ketchup and rainbow sprinkles) before deciding that, even with those enhancements, the fish was too flavorless and healthy to swallow. I sneakily let my best pal, Randy, the slobberiest Dalmatian you've ever seen, polish off the rest of my plate. He scarfed it down and thanked me with a big, wet lick to the shin. Clearly his palate is not nearly as refined as mine.

After the meal, I volunteered to load the dishwasher, which cooled Mom off a bit. As a thank you, she promised to help me outline a first draft of my final paper. We sat together at the table, pen and paper in hand. Yet my mind remained upstairs, in the depths of those volcanic rocks.

There is so much cool stuff to explore in the natural world. It's really a shame that things like schoolwork and the good fats have to get in the way.

So, yeah. I'm Malcolm, and this is my ordinary, everyday life. But ordinary, everyday life is boring. Let me get to the story.

Not just any kid can say he successfully formulated a fool-proof way of getting out of having to do homework AND saved the world by voyaging into outer space, right?

CHAPTER 2

Did I mention I'm not the biggest fan of homework? Cause I'm not.

The morning after my Mount-Vesuvius-sized meltdown, I found myself sitting in the second row of Mrs. Dawkins' fifth-grade class.

The early sun stung my eyes as I tried to force myself to stay awake. I felt sleepy after a long night spent outlining paper concepts with Mom and using every Tide pen in the house to erase blotches of food coloring/lava from the carpet.

Mrs. D stood at the chalkboard, her high-pitched voice as sweet as deep-fried Ding Dongs in caramel sauce, which I've had, and I can verify are delicious.

Mrs. Dawkins loved to inspire the class with motivational quotes, and, passing grades on her tests were as easy to earn as her smiles.

Only one thing could cause her to explode, a peeve she kept as a pet you might say—but I'll get to that (which is a concept I know to be foreshadowing thanks to Mrs. Dawkins herself). I sat with a rigid back in the chair even I'd overgrown a semester ago.

On my left, Pete Matusik played a game on his phone, aiming giant bazookas at enemies with each tap of his thumb.

On my right was Miranda Connors. She was the kind of girl a guy could have a crush on, if his time wasn't better spent becoming the next great scientific mind like Elon Musk or Robert C. Baker, the inventor of the chicken nugget.

I'd almost dozed off when Pete banged his fist into his unopened textbook, disrupting Mrs. Dawkins grammar lesson.

"No!" he blurted out—safe to assume his in-game avatar had just been blown to bacon bits.

"I don't believe this," Mrs. Dawkins said as she marched toward his seat.

Mrs. Dawkins looked down at Pete who did his best to hide his smartphone in his lap. "Peter, are we doing something we shouldn't be while we're in class?" Mrs. Dawkins asked.

She held out her hand in front of him like she was trick-or-treating.

Pete squirmed and fidgeted like he'd drank too much Mountain Dew before a long road trip, until he finally surrendered the evidence.

"Yes, I'm sorry, Mrs. Dawkins," he said, as he handed her the device. "It's my favorite game, and I—"

Mrs. Dawkins silenced him as she addressed the entire class. "Class, while I am disappointed that Peter would ignore the lecture I worked so hard on in favor of mindless gaming, I must applaud his honesty. Thank you for coming out with the truth right away."

She returned to the front of the classroom and tucked Pete's phone into her desk drawer alongside Stephanie Davis' whoopee cushion and countless baggies of Reese's Pieces she'd confiscated from me.

"You may retrieve the phone after school," Mrs. Dawkins said.

Just beyond her shoulder to the left of the chalkboard was a laminated poster of the class motto: "Honesty is the Best Policy." That's the pet peeve I'd hinted at beforehand. Mrs. Dawkins will let you get away with a lot of stuff—you just have to tell the truth if you get busted.

She trusts people instinctively, and takes them for their word without hesitating. Just don't get trapped in a fib. Believe me. I've witnessed the fallout.

Mrs. Dawkins carried on with her lesson, which today focused primarily on using the correct forms of "their," "there," and "they're." As in "there" is no chance this will ever be important to me in my real life, and "they're" out of "their" minds if they think I care about it.

I glanced around the room, hoping to spot someone or something more interesting to focus on than this snoozefest.

Near the back of the room was Marcus Mitchell, who was still undefeated in tetherball. 58 and 0!

To his right was Josh Ramsey, who had already learned four different forms of Elf languages from his fantasy novels.

And, then there was Becca Stewart, the goodiest of the two-shoes-having. She was like having a second teacher in the room, except she was even tougher than Mrs. D!

As the moments trickled past, I calculated the time remaining in class down to the millisecond. I devised an algorithm and everything. It was kind of like what a stopwatch does. Okay, it was exactly like what a stopwatch does.

I was able to pinpoint the exact moment I could pack up my dull pencil and rumpled notebook and head for the easiest class offered at this school: Lunch.

Staring at the clock, I began a countdown like I was NASA's mission control. 10, 9, 8 …. Freedom, so close I could taste it. I bet freedom's not salty enough, though. I only like really salty snacks.

Just as I began dreaming of what I might plunge my hands into during lunchtime first (I'm thinking sour cream and onion chips today), panic set in.

Becca Stewart was reaching for something.

Not her iPad, or her headphones, or even the hand of her stupid boyfriend Philip Renfrow, who wouldn't know the difference between Stephen Hawking and Stephen our school janitor.

No, she was reaching for her homework.

The vision struck me, freezing me in my tracks like Pete Matusik's blown-up video game character.

In all the chaos of the previous evening, with the outlining and the cleaning and the volcanoing (it's probably a word), I'd forgotten to do my homework.

My head bobbed back and forth at warp speed from Mrs. Dawkins to Becca to the clock to the door.

The dismissal bell was set to ring any second, and Mrs. Dawkins was, maybe, just maybe, forgetting to collect last night's homework.

After an evening spent getting an earful for soaking Mom in vinegar lava, I could use a break.

The bell dinged, and I rose proudly from my seat. Class was over.

Could I really be getting away with this? I held back a celebratory fist pump. As backpacks were stuffed and social media statuses (stati?) were updated, Mrs. Dawkins spoke over the rush of the crowd, "I will see you tomorrow, and if you have any questions, please ..."

She was cut off by an upraised hand.

Becca Stewart's upraised hand.

Upraised as in, "I have a question or statement to contribute," even though the time for questions or statements had clearly passed.

The rest of the class gathered their bags and moved toward the exit with the pace of a glacier, and I mean a regular slow glacier, not one of the ones being melted in the polar ice caps at an alarming rate.

But, I—I sped clumsily toward the door, feeling the weight of my Cinnamon Pop-Tart on top of Strawberry Pop-Tart breakfast.

With each step, I calculated the distance remaining until my escape. Adjusting for my mass and acceleration, I estimated I had about five Fruit by the Foots left to go when I heard that distinct Dawkins voice.

"Yes, Becca," she said, opening the floor.

I froze.

"I think you forgot the homework."

NO!!!!!!(To the millionth zillionth power)

CHAPTER 3

"**T**hank you for reminding me," said Mrs. Dawkins. "Please hand in last night's assignment as you leave, and remember to read through chapter three by tomorrow's class."

My stomach bubbled like a Mentos in a diet soda.

Doesn't anyone respect the bell's authority anymore? Come on, we were clearly dismissed!

I grasped for the door knob, pretending I hadn't heard her.

Head down, keep moving.

Homework? Who? What-work?

I stood at the doorframe, on the precipice of freedom and Funyuns. If I could just get a few steps further, I'd find myself along the path to the glorious land known as the lunchroom. A wonderworld filled with ice cream, sandwiches, ice cream sandwiches, and the latest issue of "Wired" (or even better, "Food Network Magazine").

I could almost smell Dorito dust wafting in the air.

Then after some serious grubbing, it'd be recess and Mr. Meyer's class (math and science—a breeze for moi), then straight on the bus home, far, far away from here. The possibility of a worry-free afternoon hung in the balance.

As I turned the cold metal knob, I pulled back on the door with all my might. And, though I'm just average height for a fifth-grader, I'm pretty strong from all the protein that's in Slim Jim's. I carry my muscle mostly in my stomach.

A cooling breeze swept across my uncombed brown bangs as the hallway became visible, an inch at a time. Floor tile by floor tile I saw my escape route open before me. When suddenly, the door jammed.

Confused, I lunged forward to increase my leverage, like when the guy at Baskin-Robbins has to crouch down to scoop overly frozen sherbet.

Yet, no matter how hard I strained, the wooden portal to joy wouldn't budge. Could this be outside resistance from an element I'd not accounted for? Had simple physics failed me?

My thoughts sped. I needed more power.

Putting my whole body into the jerking motion, I stretched my back, and as I turned, I came face-to-face with Mrs. Dawkins, whose palm was planted firmly against the door, holding it shut.

Yikes. The pressure was on.

"Excuse me, Malcolm," she said in a polite yet almost accusing tone.

"Oh, no need to say excuse me," I said, using my boyish charm. "Just on my way to lunch. Young minds require nutrients to flourish." It was a classic line I'd borrowed from Mom.

"Of course," she agreed, adding, "but, did you not hear me ask for everyone's homework?"

Words failed me, like when the doctor asks if I've been eating my five daily servings of fruits and veggies. Five?!

How could such a simple question cloud a mind as sharp as my own? I stammered out some umm's and uhh's.

The students behind meandered toward Mrs. Dawkins' desk, uniformly placing their assignments one on top of another. Miley Miller's was dotted with a heart over each "i", and Harris Roy's was crumpled like his mom had run over it in her SUV.

My classmates soon grew restless behind me as I remained standing in the doorway blocking their exit.

"Hurry up," said Bryce Smithers.

"C'mon. It's lunchtime," begged Sara Morales.

I stepped aside to let the hungry mob pass.

"My homework," I paused, unsure of where to go from here.

"Yes. I seem to have received homework from everyone but you," said Mrs. Dawkins, toe-tapping in time.

Dante Fitzpatrick sneered at me as he left, already diving into his Oreos. That's the kind of behavior that will be considered a criminal offense if I'm ever president. Peering around the room, I saw my last hope, a student as forgetful as I was when it came to the art of homework.

He sat in his chair, mesmerized by the popcorn ceiling.

"Vincent Lupard didn't do his homework, either!" I cried out.

With Vincent, it was always at least a 50-50 shot he'd forgotten, so I liked my chances. Nobody likes a tattletale, but what else could I do? This would have been like my twelfth time getting busted for missing homework. If I got grounded or something, that could mean no experiments at home for months.

"Well, that's because Vincent sprained his wrist playing Parcheesi with his aunt Meredith last night," pointed out Mrs. Dawkins. "He brought a doctor's note."

Across the room, Vincent lifted his cast-adorned left arm, signed like a championship basketball. His perfect Get Out of Homework Jail Free card.

I sighed. How do you even get injured playing Parcheesi? I must be doing it wrong.

At this point, there was no other option but to confess.

Mrs. Dawkins dove into her usual spiel. "Remember, class rules: if you forgot your homework again, I'll have no choice but to call your mother."

I could picture it all. Mrs. Dawkins phoning my mother. Mom storming up the stairs to my room, retrieving my many incredibly important science appa- ratuses (most of which I'd literally just gotten back!), boxing them up, and putting them far out of my reach high up in the garage. Then forcing me to endure weeks and weeks of nothing but homework and salmon until I convinced her I would never forget again (or until I turned 18, became a real adult, and she had no choice but to release me). It was a doomsday scenario I had to avoid.

"Well, I didn't do the homework because …," my words trailed off as two things caught my eye.

The first: Vincent's cast.

And, then: the poster that reinforced the importance of being honest in class. …the best policy.

I knew I needed an excuse, but I also knew I had to tell the truth, or face a fate far worse than a regular old missed homework grade. Mrs. Dawkins couldn't stand being misled. I replayed last night's events like they'd been DVR'd, and then an idea smacked me upside the head like when you sip lemonade that's too heavy on the lemon and way too light on the sugar.

"I didn't do the homework last night because my mom was involved in a volcano-related accident," I said with a straight face.

Mrs. Dawkins looked me up and down, not just second-guessing my story, but third, fourth, and fifth-guessing. She'd learned early on in the semester that the "take everyone at face value" strategy wasn't always a winner when it came to one Malcolm S. Webster.

"Malcolm," she said, "need I remind you of our classroom policy about fibbing?"

I held out my hands like the human embodiment of the shrug emoji. ¯_(ツ)_/¯

"I'm telling the truth. You can even call her," I said, knowing that while this was a creative version of the truth, it was still technically factual.

Deep down I knew this probably wouldn't work, but if it did, I may never be forced to do homework again.

CHAPTER 4

I've been called a genius many times. Sometimes even by other people.

Like when I discovered how to cook cotton candy in the library without crashing the school's entire computer server (third try's a charm).

But nothing compared to the praise that was showered upon me after the volcano ordeal. Mrs. Dawkins actually ended up apologizing to me!

Let me explain.

Mrs. D stood impatiently as the phone rang. With the tap of her silky-gloved finger, she turned the setting to speakerphone, which was her way of letting me hear first-hand just how toast I was going to be if this backfired. Hopefully, I'd at least be cinnamon toast, none of that multigrain garbage with birdseed all over the top.

I held in a burp, then a giggle, and did my best to fake concern for Mom's well-being, with a quiet shake of my head. "Volcanoes are super dangerous this time of year," I said, hoping May was especially magma-nificient.

Mrs. Dawkins shook her head, as if to say, "There are no volcanoes in Iowa."

Following the third ring, we heard, "Hello, Mrs. Dawkins."

Mom answered quickly, already recognizing the number, as this wasn't the first of these sorts of calls.

"Hello, yes, Mrs. Malcolm's Mom[1]. Good morning to you as well. I'm sitting here with my star science student[2], and he tells me that you were involved in some kind of accident involving a volcano last night?" Mrs. Dawkins said, getting straight to the point. And, I know what she said there wasn't technically a question[3], but I threw a question mark on the page here just to emphasize how sketched out she sounded.

In the pause that followed, I suspected there was no chance Mom would bail me out here. She liked homework almost as much as Mrs. D did. Maybe I should have blamed something else? Really, though, what's scarier than getting blasted with a face full of lava? Have some imagination, people[4]!

But, then—

"Yes, you could say that," Mom said, sounding as annoyed with me as she'd been last night, "it was a complete disaster."

I held back another fist pump. Mrs. Dawkins, remember, trusts everyone (besides maybe me).

---

1 At least, that's how I remember the conversation going.
2 Okay, this part I added myself.
3 At least according to my textbook, The Fundamentals of Grammar and Spelling v. 13.8.1.
4 Alright enough with these footnote thingies. Looking back and forth on the page is giving me a mind grain.

"I'm so sorry to hear that," said Mrs. Dawkins, feeling real remorse. "I apologize for disturbing you, and please get better soon," she added, as she hurried off the phone. Her thumb tapped the red End button just as Mom was beginning to utter a skeptical follow up that was probably also choked in confused laughter.

Mrs. Dawkins dumped the phone back into her handbag.

"Malcolm, I owe you an apology."

She patted my shoulder with heartfelt compassion, which I felt was owed to me because this was now four minutes past the bell, meaning I was already out significant fruit snack and Frito time. I nodded in agreement. "Volcanoes are scawy," I said like a baby third-grader, looking for sympathy points.

"Homework is very important, but I am glad you were there for your mom. Just bring it in tomorrow," she told me as she opened the classroom door.

I walked out of the room so quickly I was almost gliding.

"And, thank you for telling the truth," she added.

As I turned the corner toward the caf, I leapt into the air like I'd been sparked with one of those static generator balls that make your hair stick up.

No consequences after forgetting the homework? Just by bending and twisting a few details here and there?

This. This was my eureka moment, and a new hypothesis to be studied again and again—apparently, it's totally fine to not do your homework, as long as your excuse is 100% certifiably true. Or, at least, 100% certifiably not a lie.

How far could I take this? And could it somehow help me get out of writing my final paper?

I at least had to try.

CHAPTER 5

Over the next few weeks, I experimented (pun intended) with a variety of semi-plausible scenarios I could use to dodge some pesky H-Dub (which I'm told is popular kid slang for homework). They had to be valid reasons not to do any schoolwork, but not downright impossible to pull off. Tricky balance.

After school one Tuesday I found a super epic experiment online. Obviously, my assignments would have to wait. All I needed was some felt, salt water, and a stack of pennies, and I could make a working battery, which would be especially cool if any of my electronics still used old-school batteries anymore.

With some tinkering and only one mishap involving Randy swallowing a penny, I used my new trusty battery to heat up a steaming plate of peanut-butter-cup-fettucine-alfredo pasta. Delicious. Eating a dish that exquisite for dinner, midnight snack, and breakfast, I began to feel delightfully full, if maybe just a bit too sleepy to concentrate. After dozing off in first period and almost puking on my recorder during music class,

, have a

.t my home-
, tum-tum crisis

.t with an old classic
,g ate it.
,igned us to read some
, ite our own sonnets in his
for art thou, Oreo.
, from before TV even existed was
certain.   .xciting, though it could be explored
as a treat   ,or people like Mom who suffer from
insomnia. To make sure I wasn't telling a complete tall
tale, I quickly scribbled out a line or two in my notepad.
Roses are red, my favorite AirHead flavor is blue. Then I
held my camera steady as I placed the paper into the
bowl of Mr. Slobbery himself, Randy the pup.

Here's the problem. I had no idea dogs don't even
like to eat homework. It's like me with asparagus. It's
not at all a favorite food of theirs. I wish I'd known that.
I'd have written in chocolate syrup instead of pencil.

Randy was a trooper, though, and he tried one
big bite—just enough to validate my excuse as partially
true. He's the best.

I quickly rewarded him with some Pringles I had
sitting out on my dresser, which he enjoyed eating far
more than the silly sonnet. We both have great taste.

Instead of spending the evening with William
Shakespeare, I was with William Shatner, binging classic "Star Trek" episodes online. You can't beat the old
ones, but then again, I'll watch practically anything

with space, science, or aliens in it. Except "Phantom Menace".

At lunch the next day, my classmates were floored. Like many others, they couldn't believe how smart I am. No punishment for no homework? And being savvy enough to bring video evidence in to support my claim? I had significant snacktime swagger.

Tommy Brennan asked me to recount the story for a third consecutive time as I dipped a Ritz cracker into chocolate pudding.

"And then Mrs. Dawkins just bought it?" asked Roger Reddick, the fastest slow kid in school. That dude takes the "power" part of "power walking" seriously.

"Well, that's the thing, the teachers don't have to buy anything because it's all absolutely, at least partially, true. It's just massaged a little," I said, picturing myself in one of those giant leather relaxation chairs at the mall.

They rewatched my Randy-feeding footage and gasped. Pretty sure I heard more echoes of the word "genius". Maybe a "handsome" or two as well.

I wonder if Galileo had this kind of cafeteria street cred in his day.

"So, what will your next excuse be?" asked Kyle Dupree, who always seemed to have grass stains on his clothes.

I sprang up in my chair, enjoying my audience's undivided attention.

The bell rang as I prepared to boast of my latest, boldest trickery: getting out of Mrs. Dawkins final paper.

Students and teachers shuffled all around us as they made their way to classrooms, libraries, and locker rooms. I leaned in like I was telling a ghost story around a campfire. "I'm getting out of Mrs. Dawkins' end of the year paper." As I spoke a hush fell across my audience. Just saying the phrase "end of the year paper" out loud inspired fear and awe at the table, like someone had shouted the name "Voldemort" at the Quidditch World Cup. Then their faces went sour like they'd just taken a deep whiff of Kyle's grass-stained lacrosse pads.

I could sense their discomfort.

"What?" I asked them. "Do I have Sour Patch Kid in my teeth?"

Tommy pointed behind me.

I slowly turned, as the room fell silent and ominous.

Do you know how I specifically said a second ago that both students AND teachers shuffled their way around the cafeteria? Well, that was on purpose. Because at this exact moment, I turned to face none other than Mrs. Dawkins, who'd clearly just heard my grand proclamation.

She looked irritated. Maybe because instead of a lunch tray she was holding more, you guessed it, home-work. But, I think it was something else. Namely, me.

She bent down to my eye level, and I swallowed a nervous laugh.

"Yes, please, Malcolm," she said, "inform me as to why you won't be handing in the paper—the one that you've known about for pretty much all year—when everyone else does next week."

This was bad. Real bad.

I had to think and quick.

I needed something big and bold enough to justify being allowed to skip out on the term paper—yet, I would still need to be able to actually make it happen somehow (even if only by a technicality). Because with the paper due so soon, even if I started today, I'm looking at a D at best. Which would be me putting the "dead" in deadline.

Since I'd already used up some good ones, this one had to take the cake. Speaking of which, cake sounded pretty good right then.

She tapped her pencil-thin wrist with a few gloved fingers as if to say, "I'm waiting, mister."

"I'm waiting, mister," she said aloud.

Malcolm, meet Dismay. Dismay, Malcolm. Nice to meet you.

My mind swirled—Mom, Mrs. Dawkins, honesty, Randy, "Star Trek", peanut butter, chocolate, space, volcanoes, potatoes.

I shouted the next words that came to mind.

Words that were regrettable, both as a person of science, and as a person who would eventually have to make this thing actually occur in the real world. You know, in order to not get in big trouble with Mrs. Dawkins and my mom for being dishonest. And, to not have to spend the next 168 hours cooped up in my bedroom writing a boring paper.

With not a second to spare, I blurted out, "I won't be able to write it because I'm going to be abducted by aliens!"

This was going to be a doozy.

CHAPTER 6

Welp, this was going to be a problem.

Mrs. Dawkins slow-rolled her eyes and left me behind in the cafeteria. She didn't have to remind me what happens to tall-tale-tellers under her jurisdiction.

I couldn't help but flashback to the hugest, most insanely unfair punishment Mrs. D ever gave a student.

It happened back when Molly Resnick claimed that she couldn't finish reading "A Wrinkle in Time" because she was being cast to play a role in the movie.

She got busted hard when our class took a field trip to see the film, and it turned out Oprah had gotten that part.

Molly Resnick is talented. But she's no Oprah.

She got sentenced to ten weeks of detention.

Wow. Ten weeks of detention is the kind of thing that the United Nations should be working towards banning for being a crime against humanity. I'd get on that myself if I wasn't more focused on the world of science than the political arena.

This alien abduction excuse was going to take some serious work. Feeding your dog some poetry is one thing. Leaving the planet is a bit more complicated.

If Mrs. D could prove I didn't go into space, I'd get the Molly Resnick treatment times ten. I've got priors.

I'd flunk the end of the year paper, which would be pretty bad. But, even worse than the F on my report card, I'd have to spend at least the next few months without my science equipment at home. Mom would lock away my laser maze and coding books, my aqua-scope and snap circuits. Everything. Years and years spent on the Nice List down the drain. And, still, all of that would be nothing compared to the terror rained down on me from Mrs. Dawkins for being dishonest.

How many weeks of detention could she give a kid? 100? 1,000? 52 million? I could picture the future: my senior year of high school, receiving an MIT rejection letter in the mail based on a bad recommendation from my fifth-grade homeroom teacher. I couldn't afford to get caught in a lie. Science couldn't afford it either.

I decided to blow off recess. Instead, I sprinted for the library, huffing and puffing as I ran like I was being chased by a tiger snake, which would be especially scary in Iowa because they are only indigenous to Tasmania and parts of Australia. I knew this was going to require a real understanding of extraterrestrial life forms. Not that UFO mumbo jumbo you see late at night on "The History Channel".

I rammed through the doors, doing my best Kool-Aid man impersonation. "Quiet down!" our grumpy librarian yelled in a way that was in no way quiet. She must have been unaware that the fate of the scientific community was hanging in the balance. I bounded through some second-graders on the Magic Reading Carpet, and I slipped like a secret agent past our dinosaur-age computer lab.

Finally, I found a quiet corner.

I hunkered down under a stack of golden encyclopedias. These old books contained info on everything— they were like the Internet for old people.

I rubbed hard against my eyes, knowing I had a long study session ahead.

Then, I tore into a fresh Milky Way, cracked a can of Dr. Pepper (because you really can't eat a Milky Way without one), and popped open one of those fancy-schmancy volumes. The one labeled "A".

A for Alien.

CHAPTER 7

The universe is big. Like super, gigantic big.

You can see for yourself by going to your local planetarium or by streaming some "Doctor Who".

And with thousands of planets, millions of stars, and an unknown collection of galaxies, it's pretty unlikely that there isn't at least some form of intelligent life somewhere out there. I just needed to find it.

I sped-read through paragraph after paragraph of the heavy book, scanning the lines of alien references like it was a Cheesecake Factory menu.

Marvin the Martian? No. He's been too busy playing basketball with Bugs Bunny and that tall Laker guy. "Galaga", that video game that's even older than Mom? Also, no. ALF, that loudmouth from "Nick at Nite"? Don't get me started—no one likes obnoxiousness. My research wasn't uncovering anything useful at all.

"I need science fact, not science fiction," I mumbled to myself.

I swapped out the "A" volume for a copy of "S." Space—here we go. It was tempting not to stop at the entry for salami, but time was short. I'd have to come back to it. As I flipped through the pages, I noticed something. Even though reading encyclopedias isn't really my thing (and if it is your thing, please go to your nearest emergency room for a checkup), some of the satellite photos they'd included alongside the mountains of tiny print were downright incredible.

These cameras had captured mesmerizing shots of the outermost parts of our galaxy, the Milky Way. I found this especially relevant because I was eating a Milky Way at the time. I wonder if there's a Skittles galaxy somewhere.

My heart was going full Red Bull as I looked at the clock.

Halfway through recess, and still no progress.

These giant books were too textbooky. If I was going to get to space, I needed real stories of how others had gotten there. However hard to believe they may be.

I grabbed a few books off a different shelf, near where the eighth-graders passed notes about YOLOing and cooties and other such nonsense. My selections were no-brainers. "Spring Break in The Bermuda Triangle", "Finding Bigfoot in the American Midwest", and "Aliens for Dummies".

Instead of being full of dull facts and figures, these books were chock-full of kooky stories from folks who claimed to have interacted with all kinds of alien life-forms at some point. My heart believed. My sharp mind doubted. My stomach grumbled.

Unfortunately, these encounters only seemed to occur late at night, in fields, with no one around to confirm what really happened.

These eyewitness descriptions of otherworldly beings ranged, from cute little green guys to sleek gray savages. Some were tiny, like bacteria, and others were massive, like wooly mammoths. My faves were a hammer-headed taco and a taco-headed hammer.

Looking at sketches of one of the silvery, skinny dudes with daggery hands and hundreds of teeth, I couldn't decide if I wanted aliens to be real or not. I may prefer to take my chances writing the final paper.

This was going to take a lot of bravery I didn't actually have.

As I stared into its phantom face, the creature seemed to look back at me. Its eyes bulged like bowling balls.

I got the uneasy feeling that the figure was trying to taunt me from the page with mind control, when out of nowhere …

Whack!

I was knocked across the nose. My head zipped straight back.

I jolted up and assumed the double karate chop position, fully expecting the alien form to have transported itself from my page into the library stacks.

My body moved faster than my brain, making me dizzy. When my eyes finished dancing, I saw that my nemesis was not actually a space invader alien, but was instead the cartoonish, buffoonish school bully, Dennis Alsup.

His weapon of choice was a purple folder.

He pulled his arms back like an archer, readying for another bash to my forehead. "What are you studying, nerd?" he asked, in a sing-songy way that I found particularly repulsive. Dennis Alsup is evidence that perhaps not all life on Earth is all that intelligent either. His hair stuck straight up with crusty gel and glowed as bright as a Bunsen burner/Flamin' Hot Cheeto. His skateboarding sweatshirt was two sizes too large. Plus, he didn't even skateboard. To put it another way: he was the worst.

I backed away slowly. I'd never been in a fight and wasn't about to start with Dennis Alsup. He was already as tall as most of my classmates' parents, and he was arguably just as mean as the aforementioned tiger snake. I wish he was only indigenous to Tasmania, too.

I held up my empty hands, offering words of peace. "I'm not trying to bother anyone," I said.

"What kind of nerd studies during recess, nerd?" he asked, being at once both rude and redundant. Hard to achieve.

He patted the folder against his thigh for a few warmup swings. My blood boiled like overcooked Easy Mac.

I checked my surroundings for a getaway route, and as I turned to make a mad dash, my shin kicked over my latest stack of alien reads. It landed just feet in front of Dennis', well, feet. "Oh, the nerd dropped his book!" he said, bending to pick it up. "What's the nerd learning about today? How to finally meet a girlfriend?"

He opened it to the exact page that had spooked me moments before.

His face went pale as a crystal.

34

His words broke into the grunts of an Australopithecus (hope Spell Check is turned on for that one).

"Are you alright?" I asked, almost having sympathy for the simple brute.

I placed what I hoped was a calming arm around his thick shoulder, which was hardened with nerd-beating muscle.

"This is the alien my uncle saw," he said.

YES! A sign of progress. Even if it was coming from a sworn enemy like Dennis Alsup, this was my first lead.

I tried to keep it cool, despite bells and whistles going off in my head like when someone sets a new high score at the arcade.

"Your uncle saw these aliens? Where?" I asked.

"In a field, late at night, with no one around," he told me. "Mom said it's not true. She thinks it's all in his head because he went to too many Grateful Dead shows in the 70s, but I believe him. I heard his story."

The bell sounded, indicating the end of recess and quickly putting an end to our moment of unlikely companionship. I felt encouraged but rushed, as I only had four minutes to make it back to class without getting marked tardy. I couldn't waste this chance to chase down a clue.

"Can you take me to your uncle?" I asked, hopeful for a break in my case.

"What's in it for me?" he asked, stopping our sad march back toward formal education. An idea sprung upon me like an animated lightbulb had dinged above my head.

"I'm guessing you don't want to have to write Mrs. Dawkins' end of the year paper, either, right?"

CHAPTER 8

That afternoon was a blur.

I think partially because I treated myself to roughly 6.333 (repeating) of Lauren Spencer's birthday cupcakes during Mr. Meyer's class. They were chocolate ON chocolate. How could I resist?

Then again, it was probably also because my thoughts kept bopping back and forth like bumper boats.

I'd get pumped about potentially becoming the youngest person to ever win the Oppenheimer award— you know, by proving that aliens exist (by, uhh, being abducted by them). Then I'd remember what that one alien in that book looked like, and I felt like a platter of sliced deli meat. One moment I'd be relieved by the thought of not having a final paper to write, the next I'd get nervous that Dennis Alsup's uncle was just full of it. So many emotions.

Maybe it was just the cupcake crash.

Dennis and I agreed to rehash our plan on the bus ride home after last period. So instead of riding through the neighborhood dodging his spitball artillery, I found myself seated right next to the questionable figure.

He spoke with breath of fire. Seriously, it stank.

"How's this all gonna work?" Dennis asked.

I had to speak louder than I would have liked as the bus tripped and tumbled over pothole craters. "Think about it," I said. "If you and I go missing—literally disappear into outer space—there's like no chance we'd be back in time to make Mrs. D's deadline. There's no way the rest of our solar system is on our same time zone. Plus, right when we get back, the government will probably make us quarantine, "E.T."-style." I paused for effect. I leaned in closer to whisper, but had to pull back. Fire onion breath again. "And let's not forget the biggest part. If you and I prove that aliens are really real, there is no chance they could make us finish any assignments the rest of the year. Maybe the rest of ever! We'd be too busy speaking at Congress and going on "The Tonight Show" and winning science awards and stuff."

"I hope you're right. It's due in like a week," he said with a belch.

"Trust me. As long as your uncle can get us pointed in the right direction, the science savant can take it from there," I said, pointing at myself and hoping Dennis wouldn't remember that we made the exact same grade on our most recent quiz.

"I'm telling you, nerd. He can. That really scary gray one, the one from the book with all the teeth, that's the one my uncle Rod saw outside his house," said Dennis.

"I thought you said he saw them at work?" I asked, hoping this wasn't a wild goose chase after all.

"Well, he sort of repairs motorcycles in his garage, and he sleeps there. It's complicated. But, I'm telling you, he's the real deal when it comes to this kind of thing. He saw "Alien vs. Predator" like a hundred times back in the day."

I wasn't sure if I believed him, but what other options did I have?

As the mustard-colored, mustard-smelling bus trampolined over a long series of speedbumps, we finalized our agreement.

We'd meet at sundown, midway between our two homes. We'd tell no one the details, and we'd bring only what was necessary. And Dennis wouldn't pound me ever again, as long as I pulled through.

I only needed one thing: Mom allowing me out of the house. On a school night. Oh, and I guess I needed one more thing: to hope that aspiring boy-genius meat wasn't a staple of the terrifying alien diet.

I spent the next few hours gathering everything we might need for our evening off Earth. My observation notebook was a must. Same with safety goggles. And snacks. Plenty of snacks. Then I went back to reading up on who or what we might encounter in the great beyond. Martians. Apparitions. Extraterrestrials.

The table nailed my toe as Mom barged into my room just like she had on volcano night. Doesn't she ever learn?

"Dinner," she said.

She looked over my shoulders and saw a gruesome space menace on the page of my library book.

"Malcolm, you know this stuff isn't real and only scares you."

She swiped the book closed.

"Now get downstairs," she said, "I made quinoa."

Working theory: any food that difficult to spell must be terrible. Think about: Twix, Kit Kat, Buncha Crunch. Pretty simple to sound out. Quinoa? No way.

I stumbled down the stairs to the table.

I was not looking forward to explaining to Mom why I needed to skip homework for the night to go over to the house of a kid she'd never met.

And, I really wish I didn't have to mislead her. But, if this was the only way to make the story I'd told Mrs. Dawkins come true, it seemed like the least bad way to go. We sat down at our usual spots. Mom, empty chair, me. Randy warming my toes. Mom took a giant bite of that unpronounceable sand.

"How was school?" she asked.

She glopped some of her edible dirt onto my plate. Not even Randy would try a bite from under the table.

"School was boring," I told her. "Don't you think I'm ready for graduate level work by now?"

"Let's just get through the fifth-grade first," she said.

She scraped a few of her famous parsnips on to my plate. Famous for how bad they were. Parsnips and quinoa, what a combo!

She took another bite. Adult diets make me so sad.

"Anyway," she said, "how's the homework load looking for tonight?"

I cleared my throat, forcing down a smidgeon of parsnip as small as a proton. Or, a neutron. Whichever is smaller.

"I actually don't have to do any homework tonight," I said, crossing my fingers below the table. And, while this was technically a lie at the time, I knew if I could pull off my whole space alien adventure thing, it would all turn out to be true in the end. So, no real harm done.

Mom's eyebrows arched like \ / which means she didn't really believe me. "No homework?" she repeated. "Isn't the big paper almost due?"

"I know, but since we don't have to hand it in until the end of next week, Mrs. D said that tonight we should just think over the topic and ready ourselves for success." That last part I borrowed from a poster in the school gym.

"Mrs. Dawkins told you to ready yourself for success?"

"Something like that," I said. "My classmate, Dennis Alsup, invited me over tonight to brainstorm. I know it's a school night, but ..."

She didn't give me the chance to finish the thought.

"That's wonderful!" she shouted. "Did you make a new friend?"

I don't know if she wanted the TV to herself that night, or if she was just happy I was actually hanging out with other people for once, but she was letting me go! She was even excited. I couldn't believe my luck.

"I'm so happy for you. This is the growing up we talked about. Just eat a little more before you go. You've hardly touched your food, and you're normally a black hole." Ah. Mom using a science reference. I was so proud of her. Maybe one day she'll be as smart as me.

"Don't worry," I told her, picking up a piece of parsnip, "I'll be fine."

I stuffed the crummy vegetable into my mouth and held back a bit of barf.

"Just be home by 10," she said.

I kissed her on the cheek, and raced toward the door, eager to bite into something that would get this awful taste out of my mouth.

Luckily, I always have at least one Twinkie in my pocket, as any reasonable person should. I jammed that beautiful tan pastry into my mouth, and sealed the door shut behind me, just as Randy pranced outside to join me.

Dennis Alsup, Randy the Dalmatian, and me. Not exactly squad goals, but it would have to do.

It must have been dinner time for everyone else, too, because no one was on the streets. Town had fallen dark, and though I normally think most human fears are irrational—well except for vampires, those really might be real—I couldn't help thinking that everything seemed a bit spookier than normal.

The burning street lamps reminded me of the entrance to a haunted house. Every bird in the sky cawed like a buzzard circling its prey.

I spotted Dennis at the deserted corner of Bell and Walnut.

"What are you doing here, nerd?" he asked, falling back into an old habit.

"I'm meeting up with you, dude," I told him, jogging his memory.

"Oh yeah, the alien thing," he said.

Given that Dennis clearly lacked my superior intellect, I figured I should probably be in charge. "Lead the way," I ordered. Wow—me ordering Dennis Alsup around? This new me kinda rocks.

We crossed the street, and wandered along where people used to hang out in town. A dusty CD warehouse and a place where you could get a really solid bloomin' onion. RIP. Sidewalks became dirt roads that became gravel paths. Then there were more streets. Some I'd never seen before, and I've lived here all my life.

After an alleyway, we approached a graffiti-tagged garage that could be used as the setting for any of the classic horror movies Mom won't ever let me watch. A sign sprawled across the leaky roof read: "Uncle Rod's Discount Bike Repaire."

"Idiot," I whispered, "he didn't even spell Uncle right."

Dennis looked at me with a goofy smirk. He must have known I was right. We proceeded carefully up the long driveway, each of us more scared than we were willing to admit.

Unraked leaves crunched below our sneakers, and Jolly Rancher wrappers lined the dusty path, almost exactly where I'd been dropping them. Weird.

I jumped when I heard a loud _POP!_ and the wrenching of old gears.

Outside the front door, we came to a halt like we'd stumbled into quicksand. "Are you sure this is a good idea?" I asked, suspecting that this all fit firmly within the bad idea category.

"What other option is there, nerd?" said Dennis.

He was right. I hated how right he was. I just had to be brave.

"The paper's ten pages," he added.

Those words came out in slow motion. Ten pages was even more haunting than what might be behind the door to Uncle Rod's run-down barn.

My hand twitched as I held it up to knock and froze in midair.

Grunts filled the air, and heavy metal music blared at an ear-splitting pitch. Randy whimpered, intimidated.

We heard a screech and a huff and a pound.

"What's that noise?" I asked.

"I think it's AC/DC," said Dennis.

Just looking at the crumbling door made me glad I'd gotten my tetanus shots. There was no way to see inside, and it was locked shut with a corroded bike chain.

Before I could even work up the courage to knock, links began to rattle.

We scurried a few steps back. Randy crouched behind my knees.

"If it's a vampire or a criminal or something, run for it," I said.

"And if it's a nerd, I'll pound him" said Dennis, true to himself.

I exhaled like I was wishing over birthday candles. I knew this might be our only and last hope.

With a harsh groan, the door was torn open. It thrashed against the wall, then ricocheted halfway back to us.

In the shadows of the building, a fading neon sign barely lit up a graveyard of motorcycle engines and rusty tools. Standing in front of this jumbled junkyard was the roughest-looking man I'd ever seen.

He had skin like a rug burn, and a wide, angry jaw.

The freakish figure lunged toward me.

I was so scared I almost forgot I was potty-trained.

I let out a whimper as he pivoted right past me.

"Uncle Rod!" said Dennis.

They met for a hug so macho it reminded me of wild antelopes locking horns on "Discovery HD".

"What's up boys?" he cried out. "How can Uncle Rod be of assistance?"

CHAPTER 9

Uncle Rod ushered us through the front door.

From the inside, his home was about as rough to look at as he was. His only furniture seemed to be a damp futon and some empty wooden crates that originally held a soda that even I'd never heard of. There were more cracked windows than there were uncracked. We sat down on the least splintery of the old boxes.

Up close, I noticed that Uncle Rod's beard contained at least five distinctly putrid colors, like a roadkill possum. His faded tattoos looked even older than he was. And his veiny biceps told anyone who saw them, "Don't even think about messing with me."

Not even symbolically. I mean they actually said that. It was his favorite tattoo.

"What do you boys need from me?" Uncle Rod asked, "Do you want me to teach you how to talk to the ladies?"

Dennis seemed open to the idea, but my focus was purely on the task at hand: to get some useful alien intel. Plus, talking to girls—no thanks.

I mustered up the courage to bobblehead wobble my head "no."

"What is it then? Y'all got a nerd to pound?" he asked. Like terrifying uncle, like terrifying nephew.

Uncle Rod was proving to be a pretty bad guesser, so I decided to cut to the chase. "Dennis told me that you've been able to contact alien life forms, and we need to do that too."

The giant man dabbed motor oil sludge from his forehead.

"Alien life forms. Why would you wanna do that?" he asked.

"For a mission of extreme importance," I replied.

"To get out of writing a paper," Dennis followed up.

Uncle Rod shook his meaty head.

"Gee fellas, I'd love to help. But your Uncle just got out of, let's call it, Detention for Adults. And it sure wouldn't help me in terms of staying out of there, if word got out that I helped two little boys get taken away by aliens."

"Please," Dennis begged.

"I have to show Mrs. Dawkins that aliens are real," I said.

Uncle Rod cracked his thick knuckles, and walked away from our powwow back toward a motorcycle he'd been operating on.

"I'm sorry I can't help you out," Uncle Rod said.

His tone was gruff, yet apologetic. I think he really wished he could help us. "But, don't believe anybody out there who say aliens ain't real. They are real. And they're scary. Those teeth. Don't believe me? Go out back of my shop with a flashlight and some paper later tonight, and sooner or later, they'll come scoop you up."

I beamed a smile toward my unlikely companions. Randy held out a knowing paw for a human/dog fist bump.

"Tonight, paper, flashlight," I repeated, realizing that without even meaning to, Uncle Rod had just spilled the beans big time on where to find aliens in this town. Now it would be up to us to pick up those beans and turn them into something useful, like a grande burrito with pico de gallo.

Is this analogy making anyone else hungry?

CHAPTER 10

We promised Uncle Rod we'd be careful. Or that we'd, at least, keep his name out of things if and when we got busted.

Then, we tiptoed out the door, leaving our gruff guide to his wheels and wrenches. We crept around back until our ragtag gang agreed that we'd found the least ominous spot we could in the rotting field behind the Bike Repaire shop.

The three of us huddled in a small circle. I could calculate the exact area of it if I could just remember the numbers for pi. Those lessons were too distracting, though, because, well, pie ....

Pointy shrubs and wicked weeds made for an uneven seating arrangement. A not-nearly-as-cute-or-pettable-as-Randy dog rummaged through the remains of grocery bags. Tires that fit cars they no longer even build lay staring up at the stars.

We sat in silence, waiting for the first sign of alien life. Or, any life for that matter. There was straight up no one in sight.

The hushed night was only interrupted by a hungry fly buzzing and the occasional faraway Uncle Rod shout, the words of which I can't type here for fear of being sent to Detention.

Minutes passed. Then hours.

Randy moaned, in what I'm sure translated from the original Dog language into: "Just write the paper, I'm ready to go home."

Dennis echoed Randy's complaints.

"I'm tired! Give me one of your Jolly Ranchers," he said, jabbing his index finger into my chest.

"I told you, I'm out," I said, pulling out my empty pockets.

Apparently, Dennis' patience had run out at the exact same rate as my supply of hard candies.

"You told me you were helping me get out of writing it," Dennis said. "If I spend all night in this disgusting grass, and then still have to finish this paper, you better believe you're going to get pounded."

"Just trust me," I said, "this is the only plan we have for getting out of that paper. It's got to work."

I wasn't so sure.

It didn't help seeing that even Uncle Rod, the human equivalent of a vending machine playing linebacker, seemed shaken up by the mean-mouthed monster he'd met. If a guy like that was scared, I can't imagine how someone with my lack of height and spiky tattoos would feel. Though I did estimate my brain to already be significantly larger than his. Soon Randy dozed off, and I think I must have too.

In a dreamy haze, I wandered through a candy-covered fantasy world, with chocolate syrup rivers and a vanilla-filled volcano that vaporized school assignments. I hopped on a marshmallow like it was a bouncy castle, and just when I bumped into my old pals Isaac Newton (who, of course, shot fruit off someone's head and used it to make his iconic cookie) and the really smart guy from "The Big Bang Theory", I was struck in the forehead. Ouch!

"I'm awake!" I cried.

I massaged along the quickly forming bruise.

"Let's just get out of here, nerd," said Dennis. "I can still probably get home in time to sneak-watch some pay-per-view."

I didn't love the idea of staying out here all night with Dennis Alsup, but I definitely didn't love the idea of staying out here alone. So, I quickly found my footing and scampered along behind him as he hiked through the damp night.

When we reached the point where this forsaken field rejoined normal society, Randy's slobbery mouth yanked at the bottom of my jeans.

I turned to pull Randy along, when I saw the moon glowing like I'd never seen. Probably because this wasn't the moon.

This was an out-of-this-world technology space supership shaped almost like a big metal cowboy hat. Its lights were so bright you couldn't look directly at it without squinting. The vehicle was about the size of a shopping cart flipped on its side, something I've only seen once, when Mom insisted that we had ice cream at home (I knew we didn't, hence my cart flipping).

Angling its blowtorch engines, the ship dropped speed and altitude until it was just feet above us.

Then, it parked in mid-air, and a panel beneath the pod opened, and before I could even say, "Look, an alien spacecraft I can't wait to study," or more likely just "Woah," we were sucked into a vivid green beam. The strong force pulled us through the muggy night sky, onto a steep entrance ramp, and all the way into the vessel.

We entered what was equal parts a lounge and a cockpit. The cabin was stuffed with futuristic-looking equipment and seemed to be the only room on board. The driver's seat was tall and glossy like that of any good movie villain.

There was even a place near the steering wheel for snacks. Respect.

As if the ship could sense we were too tall to fly alongside the pilot's species (whatever it may be), the walls began to expand. The stylish glider went from a Kids Meal to a Super-Size, and soon the single room was the length of a super stretch limo, but with much higher ceilings.

"Woah," said Dennis.

"Ruff ruff," said Randy.

"This is incredible," I said.

Screens and buttons filled the domed insides, with more blinking lights and plastic knobs than the newest game at Dave & Buster's.

"Yes!" screamed Dennis, realizing this could easily mean 'no final paper', but forgetting it could just as easily mean 'intergalactic intruders'.

I took it all in like Christmas morning. My senses were overloaded.

I heard a blast, and we soared into orbit with speeds measured in G's, which I assume stands for "Gee, my tummy hurts."

Where us humans might have touchscreens, they had voice control. The GPS system had inputs not just for the street address, but also for planet, galaxy, and solar system. "Unbelievable," I whispered in awe.

However, the brief wonder of the moment vanished when I saw who/what was piloting our journey.

The slasher film fingers on the controls said it all.

"Welcome to Earth, new friend," I said, feeling that that was a safe option for an opening line.

Rotating the tall, leathery chair, the alien turned to face us.

Before we even saw it, an aura of dread swept over me.

The eyes were dark and deep, like you could fall through them. The head smooth and silver like a pinball. And hands that would make for a butcher's bestie.

Putting it simply, it was weird looking.

Well, that's not fair. It was weird looking for a fifth-grader.

Could be perfectly normal looking for its species of alien, though.

I'm sure I looked weird for an alien, too, even though I consider myself a well-above-average-looking fifth-grader.

The alien's look was startling. Yet, it didn't necessarily appear evil.

Then the thing stood up.

It was short, but it showed its teeth, large and sharp like tyrannosaurus talons. There must have been hundreds of them, like if a shark on steroids had eaten a shredder. Randy, Dennis, and I froze, convinced that we'd now have to face our fate as alien appetizers.

The being roared with animal violence, rumbling from its stomach through the throat and holding out both claws.

Stopping just inches from our faces, the alien opened wide and asked with a glint in its eyes, "Would you children happen to have any homework?"

CHAPTER 11

Dennis howled, "Get it!"

He bounded forward and raised his fist to throw one of his signature nerd punches; a move that was, sadly, very familiar to me.

In one fluid motion the alien wrapped two of its slimy, cucumber-length fingers around his forearm and snapped it straight back with a **CRUNCH**.

Dennis shrieked. "Wah!" he cried, like a bulldozer-sized baby. And, I must admit, hearing this under any other circumstances would have made me LOL IRL (which is the shortened Internet lingo for saying hahaha, basically the $E=mc^2$ of laughing).

The alien's mighty grip tightened around his arm, twisting it backward like a bendy straw.

Randy barked the kind of bark that would make Mom put him outside for the night. You know the one.

I looked around the room, hoping my scientific instincts would take over, but, mostly, I was just petrified.

"Please, umm, let him go?" I said, with zero certainty in my voice.

"No problem," said the alien with a smirk.

He released his tight hold on Dennis, and flung him back against the Plexiglas wall. He collapsed against the floor: shoulders, then booty, then face—all in that order. He lay twisted like a ballpark pretzel.

Dennis groaned in pain. "What's your deal, nerd?" he asked the alien. "I thought you dudes normally come in peace."

The alien's presence towered over us despite its small frame. Face cold and serious, and arms long and slithery like a mythical hydra and/or a Nerds Rope.

"While, yes, we come in peace, usually," the alien explained, "violence was provoked by you trying to punch me. I had no choice but to protect myself."

"You understand us? You speak English?" I asked in disbelief.

"Absolutely. Been using Rosetta Stone software, 30 minutes per day. Just trying to better myself, you know," the alien explained coolly.

"You didn't have to throw me so hard," Dennis whined as he crawled into a kneeling position. He'd clearly lost all confidence, recognizing that his usual tough guy routine didn't work beyond the safe confines of his home planet.

"I don't make the rules, I just enforce them," said our host, busy flicking switches and turning dials.

"Well, tell whoever made the rules they're in for a pounding," said Dennis, struggling to his feet.

I decided it was best to forget Dennis' intimidation tactics and offer the alien another friendly greeting.

Better to be on good terms with Mr. Dragonarms than not, I theorized, without even having to rely on my whiz kid logic.

I propped up my shaking hand before our captor.

"I'm Malcolm, smartest kid on Earth. And, this is Randy," I said, pointing out the pup. "What's your name? Xenon? Xenomorph?"

He spied my hand, but didn't know what to do with it.

Slowly the kitchen knife fingers found a safe resting place on top of mine. "It's Steve," he said.

Steve? Come on. There's no horror movie getting made about a spine-chilling bogeyman named Steve.

"Steve?" I asked. "Is that short for anything?"

Steve plunged himself back into his pilot's chair as he answered. "An insightful inquiry. While I go by Steve in social settings, my full legal name is Steven the Alien."

Wow. Alien names weren't as creative as I might have imagined, but I was glad he was opening up.

"Where are we headed?" I asked.

"Yeah, nerd, take us home," said Dennis.

Steve and I both shot him a glare.

"I find your compatriot most unenjoyable to be around," said Steve. "Please excuse what I'm about to do."

With that, his arms sprang forth like slinkies, grabbing rope, duct tape, and a mysterious device I'd never seen before. It was a small black box with an old-timey clothespin attached to a rotating motor.

Steve's endless arms tied Dennis up and secured his mouth tight with the duct tape. "This stuff fixes everything," said Steve.

With Dennis rendered immobile, Steve powered on the curious machine.

"What's that thing?" I asked.

Steve offered us a closer look. With a steady crank, the small engine squeezed the clothespin open and shut every few seconds.

"This is the Pinch-O-Matic 3999."

"The Pinch-O-Matic 3999?" I asked.

"Yeah, I know," said Steve, "HR wouldn't approve a budget upgrade for the 4000."

"What's it do?" I asked.

"It's going to repeatedly and painfully pinch your little friend, so that I can get on with my master plan."

Though I did agree that Dennis' attitude had earned himself a good pinching, that wasn't what I wanted to hear because master plans are always ominous. You never hear about a master plan to make the world's largest sundae or anything. It's always world domination, massive destruction, widespread chaos, blah blah blah.

"And, that plan is?" I asked, sounding hopeless.

"I'm going to take over planet Earth," he said.

CHAPTER 12

"**W**hat!" I screamed.

I think Dennis did the same, but it was so hard to tell with all that duct tape blocking his mouth. I haven't taken Rosetta Stone for speaking Duct Tape yet.

Steve confirmed our fears with an enthusiastic nod.

He tipped a joystick forward which activated the ship's overdrive.

The ship catapulted through time and space with a hibachi blaze coming out of the tailpipes.

"Reenter Earth's atmosphere," Steve spoke into his GPS. He reclined in his cockpit seat, and relaxed his long arms behind his head.

"You can't attack Earth," I said, "it's where our families live. Plus, we've got the best snacks there."

Steve prodded me with a twisted finger. The jagged poke reminded me who the captain of this ship was. I needed to keep it cool.

"Entering anti-gravity acceleration," said a programmed female voice over the speaker, robotic yet sugary.

A quick rocket boost caused the cheeks of all the Earthlings aboard to whoosh back like a Shar Pei's.

"Please, keep us safe," I begged.

Steve turned his chair to face me again. Those chair-turny things are so intimidating. I'm surprised Mrs. Dawkins doesn't have one.

He smiled at me all crooked and friendly, like an alligator breakfast-cereal-mascot would. "Well, take over the Earth may have been strong wording," said Steve. "We really just want to conquer one aspect of Earthling life."

"What is it? The economy? Energy? The global supply of Krispy Kreme's?"

Steve grinned.

"Not at all," he said. "You see, there is one delicacy that is only available on your planet. You humans take it for granted. You complain about it daily. You treat it as a burden. My people, on the other hand, love it, and in many ways, have come to rely on it."

My whiz kid brain was blended like it rode the Scrambler at the state fair. Dennis struggled with his Home Depot handcuffs as his tush took a fierce pinch. He rolled over in agony, only to take another squeeze to the kneecap. His squeals temporarily interrupted Steve's monologue.

Steve continued. "That's why we'll occasionally scoop you folks up from a field late at night. Just in hopes that one of you will have a small tote bag or even a backpack full of—"

I cut him off. "Full of what?!"

"Homework. We plan to dominate the Earth to provide our planet with an endless supply of homework."

I was so confused it felt like mymindwasliterallyhaving-amilliontinythoughtspersecondIcouldbarelykeepup.

"Mhemdjkldsio?" asked Dennis through his restraints.

"Homework is our favorite food. We thrive on it. And that's why we will be overthrowing your people."

Sidebar: what a horrible choice for an all-time favorite food. Haven't your people ever heard of root beer floats, Steve? For me, homework would probably be down there with Brussels sprouts.

"There are many more ships like mine coming. Today is the day," said Steve.

"Why today?" I asked.

Steve clicked and zoomed in on one of his hand-held screens. On it, he rewound a recording of Dennis and me scheming in the library.

"We have been studying your ways, Malcolm, and it has come to our attention that more and more students are doing what they can to avoid their homework. Much like you and Mr. Tape over there. That's why I scooped you two up tonight. I had to prove my theory. Neither of you are carrying any homework, right?"

Busted!

"If Earthlings like you are going to cease the mass production of what we love, we have to strike now."

Our ship bumped and thumped as Steve shifted the wheel. It became more difficult to keep my balance. I latched onto the wall, and out the window I noticed that we had a great view of Saturn's rings. It would have made for a great selfie if I wasn't busy uncovering a plot against humanity.

"Arming weapons," said that same lady's voice.

I hated that sound. It was oddly like I'd heard it before, but I couldn't place it. "Missiles preparing to fire," she added.

"Missiles? Woah, woah, woah. Don't you think this is all going a bit too far?" I asked.

"Your society has controlled the homework supply for far too long. Math problems, spelling flashcards, dioramas. It's not fair. We will take our share, even if that means taking the Earth as well," said Steve.

By now, any hopes I had for survival were all but ~~crossed out~~.

The Pinch-O-Matic 3999 struck again on the loose skin of Dennis' elbow. Randy barked desperately, this time in the alien's native language. I couldn't tell you where he picked that up. Pupcasts cover every topic these days.

With a mind control flip of the wrist Steve tangled Randy in the same mess of a trap that Dennis was in. Pinch-O-Matic and all.

I prepared for the worst, though I had to admit that mind control skill would be pretty sweet to have for when you forget to grab extra ketchup for your fries.

"Missiles aiming for Earth," said the voice from above.

I looked to Dennis, then to Randy.

Then I kind of just blurted out the first thing that came to my mind, like when you Tweet on a sugar high.

"You don't have to take the whole Earth! Just take my school!"

Steve considered this for a moment. "Your school?"

"Yeah," I said, "we've got more homework than anyone knows what to do with. And, that'll be less messy than a war with the entire planet, you know."

"You're telling me your school has a virtually unlimited supply of homework available every single day?"

"That's right. It's like Olive Garden breadsticks. Plus, we're nearing final paper season next week. 10-15 pages. Per student."

Steve's eyes lit up. *Per student.*

He rotated his chair back and began punching buttons on his computerized TelePad. While he was distracted, I bent down.

"Just going to tie the old shoes," I said, but joke's on Steve, I wear Velcro's. According to Mom, they're even cooler than being able to tie your own shoes.

Reaching just past the tip of my toe, I grabbed the base of the Pinch-O-Matic 3999. "New destination confirmed. Recalculating route," said the robotic lady.

"This will be perfect," said Steve, "No intergalactic warfare, and homework for everyone! Simply by toppling one tiny school. A celebration!"

Steve turned to, I guess, thank me, when CLAP!

The clothespin pincher found a new home right on the base of Steve's stubby nose. He slipped and slided, and I rope/duct tape entwined him like he'd done to Dennis. Then I darted away, looking for something, anything, I could use to fight back.

CHAPTER 13

I knew I'd have to do more to fend off Steve. After all, what I'd hit him with wasn't even the latest model of Pinch-O-Matic. It could only hold him back for so long.

Saving my hometown, my classmates, and yeah, my school, from a cosmic crushing rested solely in my greasy hands.

I Usain-Bolted for the only place I figured could help save the day.

Far at the other end of the long hall of the ship.

The area my alien ride had turned into his make-shift kitchen.

The kitchen always saves the day.

I huffed and puffed, streaking (not the naked kind) along the narrow walls. I could hear Steve struggling to regroup behind me. A mighty pulse broke the pinching device from his shriveled nose. He threw the machine like a PE dodgeball, a perfect strike that locked into place on Dennis' groin.

Bullying is never cool, but after that spectacle, it was hard not to have at least some sympathy for the guy. His soprano screeching shook the slick disco-ball floors. I barreled into the fridge like a nearsighted gorilla on roller-skates.

This wasn't exactly a spacious kitchen like the kind that makes Mom jealous when she watches "HGTV". It wasn't even as built out as the one I'll someday have in my dorm at Harvard. But it would have to do.

I rifled through the cabinets like airport security searching for the can of Yoo-hoo I'd left in my carryon. At first, I didn't recognize most of the stuff in the cupboards. Beyond the basics, it was like aliens had their own food system.

Homework-flavored chewing gum. Homework-flavored jerky. Homework-flavored baked beans.

So, this must be what Steve was talking about. Their people love the stuff.

Me? I've got a pretty impressive appetite, but I think even I'd draw the line at homework-flavored baked beans. No thank you.

Food packages rocked from the shelves as my clumsy arms tornadoed items to and fro. Mostly fro.

I heard a harsh ripping sound like underpants splitting at the seams. I turned to see Steve's chainsaw cuticles tearing the rest of the rope and duct tape into confetti. He tossed a handful into the air in defiance, mocking our attempt to confine him.

"Stop, fool," Steve cried out toward me, as he parked himself in the cockpit once again. "You really think you can save your planet, or even your school?"

Now, of all the places on Earth that could get detcimated (that's when you get detonated and decimated at the same time), my school wouldn't be the worst option. I mean, it is still a school. Better that than the Auntie Anne's at the mall.

Yet you've gotta figure, even someone as bright as me may one day be looked down upon if they never technically got a middle school diploma. So, in that respect, saving it could be an investment in my future boy genius activities.

Plus, there are probably some pretty nice perks available to anyone who spares humanity from utter ruin. Think about it—you can't make the guy who saved the entire species from annihilation fork over cash for an ice cream cone. That's just not right.

Steve's war cry crackled through the overhead intercom.

"Calling for further reinforcements. Change of plans. All fighter ships meet at Malcolm Webster's grade school. We'll confiscate their homework supply then blow the place to smithereens."

Steve then fired a foul-fart-face my direction.

"Then we can reconsider the whole world domination thing," he added.

Here's a complete list of everything in the known universe scarier than someone calling in reinforcement alien fighter ships:

1. Nothing. Not even one thing.
2. Yeah, I still got nothing.

There was no time to freak out or make lists, though.

Steve BOOMED our cowboy-hat-hot-rod faster. Then faster. Then, I think even faster than that, but it's hard to say because I was woozy like I'd been used as someone's personal piñata. The ride felt like taking a spin on the Gravitron after a half-gallon of black coffee. My dizzy forehead clunked into the spice rack, when it dawned on me—

Even an alien as cunning as Steve needs to be able to see where's he going. Otherwise, he could get take a wrong turn or get a Space Ticket from a Space Cop.

I grabbed a bottle of vinegar and the rest of his alien baking soda, wielding one salmon-recipe-staple-turned-samurai-saber in each hand.

I cracked my neck, let out a rhino snarl, and did a highlight reel-worthy 180° to face that horrible homework hog.

Then, I charged him.

"Dun, dun, dun," I said to myself, immediately realizing, that yeah, that was a pretty dorkish thing to say.

CHAPTER 14

I bounded toward Steve's pilot chair.

I don't know where all this bravery was coming from. It's almost like people are capable of incredible personal developments when they're hoping to dodge their responsibilities.

"Please, Steve," I screamed with high-pitched intensity. (Hopefully my voice will eventually get deeper. It better. It's hard to intimidate a guy whose fingertips could filet you when you sound like a talking toy pig or something.)

"Don't make me do it," I cried, as I steadied the vinegar and baking soda containers in my hands. I knelt next to my backpack and tore open my observation notebook, rifling through the pages like holiday wrapping paper until I landed on the recipe for the Mega Volcano. Then, in my head, I quadrupled it.

"Entering Earth's atmosphere," said Steve over his intercom.

"Confirming backup," said that female voice again. It was getting more familiar each time it spoke. Was it … *Mrs. Dawkins*? Is that crazy?

I could now see these backup ships outside each glass panel. A collection of the cowboy hats. Plus, a horde of hovercrafts. A myriad of mechs. A fleet of flame floaters. And one robotic bunny rabbit for whatever reason.

Steve crammed a lever all the way down which thrusted us forward. As I stumbled back, I tapped his shoulder.

He turned to face me.

"Sur—!" I cried out, as I dumped the bottle of acid into the powdery base. I was trying get a full "Surprise!" in, but I kind of got ahead of myself.

Like an over-shaken Sprite, fizz frothed from the container, salty and cloudy. I aimed the spray right between Steve's two black face-bullets.

Bubbles burst into Steve's mouth and eyes. His sharp hand-scissors reached to wipe away the blinding foam.

"My eyes!" he said, rubbing them with his palms like he was trying to stay awake during a grammar lecture. "It stings!"

Steve toppled onto his side, wailing in alien agony. I moved quick to untie Randy from his homemade jail cell. I tore the tape from his lips, which he thanked me for with a lick on the leg. Randy did the smart thing, which was to immediately bite Dennis free from his binding. He knew we'd need some muscle.

Steve dove for me, but his blurry vision made him miss. He came down in a fresh pool of Randy slobber.

What a lame strategy. I mean, he couldn't even see me. He flopped around the floor like a fish on an ice-skating rink.

With no one at the steering wheel, the ship began to plummet. Full velocity, with no control over our direction, headed for Crashtown, population: us. We weren't even using our blinker.

Facing down a g-force fender bender, I had no other option—I climbed into Steve's seat. "Brave, brave," I reminded myself between hurried breaths.

Steve leaned against the wall as he tried to stand. Seeing a weakened target, Dennis Alsup flexed his newly-freed fingers. He then proceeded to give Steve one of the worst noogies I've ever seen.

"Ahh!" Steve said, as his scalp was noogied mercilessly.

"Mechsmemds," said Dennis. At this moment, I realized I'd not yet removed the duct tape from his big mouth, but I decided to maybe keep it on him for an extra minute or two to savor the moment.

I gripped the wheel tight like a PS5 controller, doing my best to steer this piece of weaponized Western Wear. I'd have to lean on every driving technique I'd picked up at Bumper Car Village to keep this thing steady.

"Please, no," Steve begged, as his bald head was grinded by Dennis' rough knuckles.

Randy leaped in to help ward off our adversary, contributing a tongue-tickle-torture of his own, that might have ended a lesser species.

Steve both laughed and cried, as I cheered them on.

"Don't mess with Earth!" I said, hoping it would come out cool like an action movie hero, but it was not all the way there. I'll need to work on that.

Between giggles and tears, Steve was able to rush out a few words.

"Please! We're going to crash. Stop this madness. I will pardon your school, if you just stop! Now!"

I looked at Randy, who looked at Dennis, who looked at me, who looked over at that snack pantry. I was getting hungry, and maybe homework-flavored jelly beans aren't so bad.

"You call off the reinforcements, and we will let you go in peace," I said, realizing we were headed straight for an on-time arrival at the scrap heap, if we didn't right the ship ASAP. Steve held out his mangled paw of a hand.

"Deal," he offered.

"Deal," I said.

Holy bologna. I did it. Or, so I thought.

I slid to the side of the seat, and allowed Steve to grasp the controls. Though I was careful to keep the vinegar and baking soda in hand in case he got all crafty on me again.

"Calling all fellow fighter ships," Steve said, "abort plans to attack Malcolm's school. I repeat, abort attack plans. Hold all fire as we approach. Upon arrival, leadership will reconvene on an alternative plan."

Steve gasped, still nursing his eyes back to health.

"That stung quite forcefully. Where does one begin to master creating such an unstoppable concoction of a weapon?" Steve asked.

That's when it dawned on me. The first time I ever built that volcano was for a homework assignment. That's where I learned it. Homework.

Wow. Could it be? Homework—not so bad after all?

I mean if it can basically teach you how to fight off aliens, maybe there is something to it after all.

Eh. I doubt it.

CHAPTER 15

Steve settled in behind the wheel. His cool demeanor (or should I say, *chill vibes*?) made it clear he'd come to terms with our negotiations. Yet, we were still surrounded by ominous ships on all sides. Their lights and gadgets shined like infinity. And, up close, I could see that they each had their own supply of heavy explosives perched at the ready like angry pterodactyls.

Stuck between calm and chaos, I took a few deep breaths, gazing out the window upon the wondrous mystery that is outer space. The Earth was a shiny blue marble, flickering with lights in the night, and its many mountain ranges that looked like Milk Duds from here. At least half the planet seemed fast-asleep.

That's when I realized, I had no idea what time it actually was on Earth. How long had we been venturing through space anyway?

"What time is it, Steve?" I said

"Ahh, time. Such an Earthling construction," he sighed. "All aspects of time and space are relative, when you consider the continuous expansion of matter and the ongoing transfer of ..."

"Answer the question, nerd," said Dennis, peeling off his own mouth-muffler. Steve hissed back with a forked tongue.

"Easy now," I said, holding my salmon recipe weapons before me. "There will be no nerd punching or bully eating," I assured my co-passengers.

Dennis pouted, but Steve quickly withdrew his tongue.

Our GPS blinked and blipped. The on-screen destination read: Malcolm's School. Wow. I can't believe how specific alien GPS systems can be.

We passed rivers and plains. We passed a McDonald's, but Steve refused to hit up the drive-thru window, no matter how nicely I asked.

We dropped altitude as we approached a soft, warm landing spot on Earth. A green and lush field perfect for the regular kids to play sports on while I hit the 'boratory (short for lab, duh.)

I finally relaxed. I propped my feet up on the dash, and the sun's early rays glittered in my eyes.

"This is great. I'm gonna be famous, I'm not going to have to write my paper, and it's a beautiful morning for Fruity Pebble waffles," I said.

Wait, *morning?!*

"Steve! It's morning?" I asked.

"As I said, time is a relative concept. However, if you must know, given our current coordinates, it is now Earth-time 8:23 a.m.," Steve said.

Uh to the oh. I was going to be so busted. We'd stayed out all night! What was Mom possibly going to say about this? We'd gone completely MIA. Taking over an alien pod or not, you have got to call your mother. Or at least, shoot her a text.

"We need to get to school, NOW," I screamed.

"Approaching Malcolm's School," said the overhead intercom lady. Her perfect timing was getting annoying.

"Fasten those seatbelts and stow your tray tables for landing," said Steve, plagiarizing Southwest Airlines, I suspect.

We held on tight as the ship tumbled and fumbled toward the Earth. We did a barrel roll, and I still can't tell if that was a necessary maneuver to ensure a safe landing or was just Steve showing off his piloting skills.

The space ship more thudded than parked smack-dab at the center of our school's soccer field. Its powerful engine left scorch marks along the goalie box, much to the dismay of the groundskeeper Mr. Martin, who hadn't changed his hairstyle since the late 80s. He waved his arms like we cut him off in rush-hour traffic.

As the glass lid to the ship popped open, the intercom lady spoke up again. Always interrupting.

"Calling all ships: school attack engage," she said.

"School attack?! Hold on. I thought we had this all figured out," I said.

"Too late to cancel operation," said AIL (my shorthand for Annoying Intercom Lady).

"Does this mean we are going to have to fight?" asked Dennis. "Cause I'm happy to pound a nerd or two."

"Steve, help," I said, still focused on maintaining peace between our species. The sky turned gray under a wave of incoming visitors. Their wings blanketed the morning in a vast, steel nightmare. They clearly missed the memo on trading interspecies hostilities for free homework.

Steve stood and placed his slimy-disgusting hands on our shoulders. One on mine, one on Dennis'. Not sure why he snubbed Randy.

"Of course, peace is the priority. But if we must fight, we will fight. You are a man of honor, Malcolm. If you can provide the homework you've promised, I will defend your school. Even from my own people," said Steve.

He ejected his claws like Wolverine. I grabbed my vinegar and baking soda. Dennis picked up what was left of the Pinch-O-Matic. Randy yelped like a good boy gone bad.

"We've got a planet to save," I said.

We stepped through the open rooftop into the blistering sunlight.

Just then, the first fireball barrage struck down through the clouds. The blast missed us badly, but squashed a Subaru or two instead. We huddled behind a lamppost. "Steve," I asked, "just curious: how delicious is homework to you guys?"

"Better than any Fruity Pebble waffle you've ever had," he answered.

With that, I was washed over with guilt. I can't imagine living on a planet without my go-to snacks. How could I expect the aliens to?

I spoke again. "Listen, I don't blame you guys for doing whatever it takes to access the best food that's out there. I'd probably do the same for some Twizzlers.

Just get them to stop Charizarding us, and I'll make sure you have all the homework you'll ever need."

The bell must have rung. Or, maybe it was the sound of sedan explosions. But, soon we had a giant crowd of my classmates surrounding us. I suppose after seeing our spacecraft, they kind of gave up on the whole "going to class" thing to come see what was going down.

Beth Patterson, Beth Bishop, and the other Beth. Luke Spears, who practices steel cage wrestling moves on me regardless of if I'm playing along or not. Drew Parker, whose mom makes the best brownies in four counties—which I know to be true, because I've sampled every brownie in four counties.

The student body broadcasted us facing down our from-a-galaxy-far-away-guests on every smartphone app known to mankind (or alienkind). Steve, Dennis, Randy, and I cowered before the hammer-headed taco and the taco-headed hammer on PinTokGram, SnapFace, and everywhere in between. I admittedly didn't look my bravest while keeled over begging for mercy or one final donut, but their streaming footage did go viral in seconds—which was a huge win for my alien abduction alibi, and would go on to became a hilarious meme both on Earth and on Steve's planet.

Eventually even Mrs. Dawkins found her way outside, and she is never late for second period.

As the robot bunny and the jet fighters taunted the student body with aerial acrobatics, Steve looked truly scared. How could he not be? We were face-to-face with mutilation-ready masses. Plus, he'd just stepped foot on Earth for the first time and was already trending on social media as #SchoolSpaceShip.

"Steve, remember. We want peace. We all do. My school alone has hundreds of homework assignments, of varying quality, handed in every single day. We can partner together, and make sure that it all goes to a good place and your people never have to go without," I said.

"Malcolm, you see, that plan only works if you and all the other students actually complete the homework assignments in the first place. No more juvenile excuses," said Steve.

I wish he wasn't so right. "Yeah, I guess," I said, reluctantly.

Steve winked at me with his hollow, glowing eyes. It was a pretty sickening gesture but I think he meant it well.

He motioned his arms up to the sky like an orchestra conductor, welcoming the flame-throwing foes to join him in this homework-happy-place. He smiled and waved with contagious energy. I nearly joined in.

But, just when progress seemed possible, the sound of approximately 8 trillion (give or take 7.99 trillion) alien ships loading their rocket launchers CRUNCHED through the air like a bite into a petrified pita chip.

CHAPTER 16

I held tight to my baking soda and vinegar like my life depended on it. Which I guess, technically, it did.

The apocalypse was here, and it smelled like monster truck exhaust with a side of monster diaper.

My teammates flexed with their weaponry as well.

Randy twirled his tongue, stretching his lips wide for maximum ticklage.

Dennis chomped with the broken pieces of the Pinch-O-Matic, just hoping he could get a bite or two out of what was left of the device. Discouraged, he threw it to the floor, and pummeled his fist into his open palm, warming up his best nerd-punching hand.

Steve sharpened his one set of finger claws with his other set of finger claws.

"Let's do this!" I shouted.

I reached over and hit the Play button on the radio aboard Steve's ship. We would need a killer soundtrack if we were going to stand a chance. I tuned the dial to A-Rock, 107.7. And, ladies and gentlemen—I definitely recommend Alien Rock next time you need to defend your hometown from barbarians or hang glide off a mountain with a crossbow. It gets you PUMPED. What's it sound like you ask? Imagine if a marching band made up entirely of untrained second-graders tried playing an Imagine Dragons song while being chased off the edge of a waterfall by rabid hyenas.

It rocks.

The robot rabbit stomped through the school-yard, and SMOOSHED the library's roof into a penny. Hovercrafts floating overhead dropped baby bombs that did their best to turn Mr. Martin's soccer field into a full desert landscape. The ground was cooked. Sautéed even.

Fighter jet lasers blasted through the sky, vaporizing textbooks and lighting backpacks aflame. Rockets shattered windows and threw picnic tables 80 feet into the air. Kids and teachers scattered for cover, abandoning their front row view of the ridiculous ruckus. They must have figured they'd be able to catch the rest of the footage live on Twitch. I dumped the last glugs of vinegar into the baking soda, but my bubbles and fizzies were no use as the space ships glided back and forth overhead. I threw the empty container, and actually hit something with a light DOINK. Unfortunately, vinegar bottle DOINKS don't do a whole lot to harm interdimensional metal pods. It cruised by unscathed.

Steve clawed the rabbit robot. Its metal bodysuit **CLANGED** against his machete manicure. My alien ally stretched his arms like a boa constrictor, and pushed the mech into the ground until its battery puttered out. He then hoisted the bad boy bunny overhead, and boomeranged it through three of his cowboy hat frenemies—giving their rides extra sunroofs they never asked for.

An alien that looked like an even grumpier version of Steve opened his pod's glass shielding. He chucked something down at us. A weapon? A bird? A plane? No, it was the Pinch-O-Matic 4000. Indeed, it was quite an upgrade from the 3999 model I'd seen before.

The squeezing machine landed just behind Dennis, and gave his booty one of the sharpest grabs I've ever witnessed. Brutal.

"My butt!" he screamed.

Our loud librarian marched over and gave him a detention slip.

"You may not say butt on campus, Mister," she said, "even when you're fending off legions of laser beams."

Dennis collapsed to the ground. He then resumed his complaining, now being extra careful to only use school-approved terminology to describe where he'd been injured. "My tuchus! My hiney!"

The squadron of evil Steve-lookalikes paused in mid-air. They teased us with their powerful blasters and laughed to themselves like a possessed live studio audience as we ran for cover.

"Look at that one kid who tried to stop us with baking soda and vinegar," said one alien.

"Yeah, is he defending Earth or making salmon?" said another.

I screamed for help until my lungs felt like ice. I cried out for the police, Batman, Mom, anyone! Yet my words were no use, as they were buried in the sounds of anti-gravity motors and alternative rock music from lightyears away.

I ducked under what was left of Steve's spaceship to take cover. I ran some quick numbers and concluded that, statistically, I was at least 42% less likely to get broiled like a Whopper if I was hiding under the base of a ship.

A blender-fist with a bad attitude jumped me from above. His razor fingers spun and moved on their own like scorpions. He held a fingernail like a fang to my cheek, as I pushed back on his slimy skin with all my might. He flashed his many teeth, showing that he wasn't a huge fan of dental floss and that he had zero reservations about eating me whole. I head-butted (apologies, I meant head-tuchus'ed) my blocky nose into one of his demonic eyes. "Prepare for alien arrival," said that rehearsed intercom voice.

"Roger that," said an alien, who I later found out was named Roger. Weird. The rest of our combatants lowered their vessels, draining speed as they inched closer to my school's campus.

Giant bots hosted a homerun derby with the remnants of the art building. An alien lava laser singed off all of Dennis' hair. Bald was not a great look for him.

"Confirming alien arrival," said Roger.

"No! Not alien arrival! Prepare for alien peace," SCREAMED a voice, familiar, yet difficult to place. Its presence felt much closer than the words of the intercom, but its inflection was the same.

Steve spun around, eager to identify who that voice of reason belonged to. You could tell he knew that sweet sound from somewhere. The rest of us turned as well—all of us who hadn't run for their lives or been flung a quarter mile away by a 60-foot toaster alien. Did I mention there was a 60-foot toaster alien? Cause there was.

Through the rubble of a shrapnel-encrusted auditorium, Mrs. Dawkins drew near. She paced through remnants of the melee, holding a giant sack.

As she climbed past a crater and over our beat-up school bus, she dug into the large bag. Jerking her arm up and back, she pulled out sheets and sheets of paper. *What the what?* Paper? Where's your weapon, Teach? Thought we were trying to safeguard the school here!

Mrs. Dawkins spread the white sheets among the fray, tossing them left and right like a wedding flower girl gone mad.

The alien who was seconds away from prying my eyes out and downing them like cocktail meatballs let go of my arm. His spring-loaded wrists whipped to the ground, and grabbed a stack of the documents from a still-burning patch of grass.

He shuffled through them like he was speed-opening birthday cards trying to locate the cash within.

From my vantage point, I could see it all. Grammar exercises, spelling quizzes, lab reports, social studies assignments, and more.

The fighting froze. The alien shed a toxic tear.

Silence fell over the school yard. Wait, who turned off the A-Rock? That was my jam. The alien forces stood still, mesmerized by the bounty Mrs. Dawkins offered. My homeroom-teacher-turned-hero stood high upon Steve's ship.

"Stop this madness, there is another way," she said, flinging the rest of the homework up toward the alien school-crashers. She emptied her big bag like the world's saddest Santa. Then Mrs. Dawkins took her gloved hand and pulled off her Mrs. Dawkins mask.

CHAPTER 16.5

Wait, *what*?!?!?!?! ?!?!?!?! ?!?!?!?! ?!?!?!?! ?!?!?!?! ?!?!?!?! ?!?!?!?! ?!?!?!?! ?!?!?!?! ?!?!?!?! ?!?!?!?! ?!?!?!?! ?!?!?!?!<MLP2Q21~"LKM@2 (sorry, spilled maple syrup on the keyboard—I meant to type more ?!?!?!?! ?!?!?!?! ?!?!?!?! ?!?!?!?! ?!?!?!?! ?!?!?!?! ?!?!?!?!)

CHAPTER 17

Huh? I've never seen a Mrs. Dawkins mask at Costume City. Or even in a monster movie.

Could it really be?

It could be!

Her pasty skin and curly hair came right off to reveal, a smooth gray face, that looked almost exactly like—

Steve hugged her. He recognized her instantly.

"Mrs. Dawkins," said Steve. I couldn't believe that was also her alien name. "I haven't heard from you since you left the outer space voiceover industry!"

Mrs. Dawkins addressed the audience.

"Yes. Please listen, fellow aliens (she actually said their species' name, but it can't be typed in our letters—something like Σ¡|_\/ëR Æ|_¡ëŃ). I came to this planet years ago to safely and peacefully have access to unlimited homework. I believe we can all do the same. By maintaining a healthy, working relationship between our peoples, this school can educate the Earth's youth while also supplying us with all the tasty, nutritious homework sandwiches and homework pie they could ever want."

Homework pie didn't sound that bad—I'll give them that.

The crowd applauded like wild. They parked/landed their ships all over what was just the scene of a middle school massacre. Celebration ensued.

Like a waiter at the fanciest restaurants in town, Mrs. Dawkins served every alien in sight a fresh piece of homework, boiled down into the same mush-like substance I'd seen her eating at her own house that time. They savored each bite like it was a chicken tender with another chicken tender wrapped around it.

Steve used his ship's super chargers to heat up a few of the papers. The sugary smell of caramelized chemistry lessons lingered in the humid air like fresh bacon. Wow, that was poetic. I must be hungry, too.

It all made sense to me now.

No wonder Mrs. Dawkins was so obsessed with assigning homework. She was an alien herself!

And, it turns out these aliens were totally open to peace between planets. They just get a little angry when they run out of good grub, which anyone can relate to.

For reasons I'll likely never be able to explain, I walked over and embraced Mrs. Dawkins with open-arms, like we were BFF's. I guess I had to thank her for saving my handsome face and giant brain just then.

"I told you I wasn't lying about outer space!" I said, gloating just the tiniest bit. She gave a sly nod, tugging her mask back into place.

"Does this mean I can officially skip writing that final paper?" I asked.

"I don't think so. We're starving," she said.

We all belly-laughed like a bad laugh track.

The aliens piled the excess homework onto their only-slightly-damaged ships, and agreed to politely stop in once per week to collect an all-you-can-eat buffet of our learnings. Steve and I wished each other farewell. I promised to try his homework casserole next time he came to town, so long as he'd help me out with the occasional science fair project. Which I'm absolutely going to take him up on. He was, after all, a space genius with technology from the future.

With that, the alien invaders were gone just as soon as they had arrived. I even had to go straight to second period.

It was a bummer to spend the rest of the short semester in a mostly burned down school that had been attacked by aliens, but at least no one got hurt too badly. And, plus—I had prevented the entire planet from getting blasted into oblivion. Which made me like a hybrid action hero science master. Think Vin Diesel mixed with ... Uh, I can't think of any more famous science people. Vin Diesel mixed with the smartest teacher Vin Diesel ever had.

Sure. Hearing this story yourself, you may think some of this mess was at least partially my fault. But, I mean, how upset can you be with the guy who a) did not actually tell a lie and b) showed the whole world that aliens exist? I rest my case. Really, it ended up being more of a "not mad, just disappointed" situation.

Not even a full week later, I showed off my newfound maturity and appreciation for homework by writing every last bit of the dreaded final paper. It was titled, "How Different Species Enjoy Snacking," and Mrs. Dawkins handed it back to me the next morning with a big, red "A-" scrawled across the top.

We celebrated by taping that triumphant first page on the refrigerator door—the rest of the paper became a tasty tempura-battered hors d'oeuvre courtesy of Chef Steve. A true win-win.

So, hey. Getting a pretty awesome grade on the big paper project, being super brave while keeping Earth from the brink of destruction, and having a verifiably legendary scientific discovery to my name all before entering middle school?

Maybe I'm no longer just an aspiring whiz kid.

Maybe I'm the real deal.

CHAPTER 18

So, yeah, this is the new normal.

Turns out, things aren't that different, even after you save the world.

I haven't won my Nobel Prize yet (somehow.) But, I'm still Malcolm, and I'm still crazy about science. I may even make a B in it next year. At least that's what one of those Jimmy's from late-night TV said.

Mrs. Dawkins still gets upset with me when I forget the homework. At least now I understand why. Hanger is real, y'all.

Mom still gets on my case about not listening to her. At least that's what I think she said. I wasn't really paying attention.

We even had dinner together right before I started telling this story. She made, *ugh*, salmon, but she remembered to serve the chili cheese pudding sauce on the side. So, it was edible. Barely.

Sometimes I even sit in Dad's old chair right next to Mom while we eat. This new bravery thing's working out.

And, through all this, I learned a valuable lesson. Homework's important because if you don't do it, you can't end up going into outer space and saving the world from absolute annihilation.

I think Dennis even learned something as well: only threaten to pound things with less than 400 teeth.

But learning lessons is boring.

Let's do some science!

"Experiment time!" I called out to no one in particular.

Luckily, Steve is still just a short space blast away anytime I need his help with anything. "Get ready to solve a food crisis, Steve!" I said, strapping on my goggles. My alien pal bounded through my bedroom window like a new puppy.

"Indeed, it's experimentation time," he said.

"With your help, I'm going to create the first synthetic homework food product. We'll forever change the snacking game! Well, your planet's snacking game," I said.

"Let's do it," said Steve.

We high-fived, which was more like a high-twelve with Steve's scary looking hand. I grabbed a beaker, and Steve hooked a clipboard from the shelf.

"By the way," I asked my new pal, "when am I going to get to visit your home planet?"

He thought about it.

"Maybe when you're in sixth-grade," he said.

YES!

I slammed the door to give us that authentic lab setting. And, just then my mom shouted, "No science until I see that you've finished your homework!"

"Homework. Hmm. Where did I leave that again?" I muttered to myself.

I looked at Steve.

"You hungry?"

THE END.

Enjoy the read? Let others know by leaving a review! And, stay tuned for more of Malcolm's adventures coming soon to an online bookstore near you.